THE GOLDEN COMPASS™

THE OFFICIAL MOVIE
QUIZ BOOK

LISA REGAN

■SCHOLASTIC

ISBN-13: 978-0-545-01614-8

ISBN-10: 0-545-01614-2

Published by Scholastic Inc.
SCHOLASTIC and associated logos are trademarks and/or registered trademarks of Scholastic Inc.

12 11 10 9 8 7 6 5 4 3 2 1   7 8 9 10 11 12/0

Editorial Director: Lisa Edwards
Project Manager: Neil Kelly
Project Editor: Laura Milne
Designed by Aja Bongiorno

Printed in the U.S.A.
First printing, November 2007

Contents

Introduction

Welcome to the incredible world of *The Golden Compass*. . . .

Within these pages you'll find hundreds of brain-teasing questions based on *The Golden Compass* movie. Split up into different themes, each quiz includes easy, medium, and hard questions, all of which are guaranteed to test your knowledge of the extraordinary world depicted in this spectacular motion picture.

The Official Movie Quiz Book includes questions on the alethiometer, the feisty heroine Lyra Belacqua, and the many intriguing characters she meets on her remarkable odyssey, including terrifying Ice Bears and beautiful witches. Towards the end of the book is the "Inner Dæmon" challenge, where you can find out which animal form your own dæmon would take.

So, what are you waiting for? Read on to begin your very own quest into the unknown. . . .

Lyra's World

How much do you know about the strange and wonderful world that Lyra inhabits?

1. What is a person's soul known as in Lyra's world?

2. What does Lyra call Lord Asriel when we first hear about him?

3. What is the name of Lyra's dæmon?

4. What does Lyra tell Mrs. Coulter about the death of her parents?

5. How old was Lyra when her parents died?

6. What are the Panserbjørne also known as?

7. What kind of animal does Mrs. Coulter have as her dæmon?

8. Who is John Faa?

9. Who are the Samoyeds?

10. When does Dust start to form around people?

11. Who is Iorek Byrnison?

12. What is Iorek Byrnison's armor made from?

13. Who is Lyra's best friend?

14. What country does Lyra live in?

15. How long do witches live for?

16. Whose dæmon is a hare?

17. Where is Bolvangar?

18. Who is Lizzie Brooks?

19. How does Dust enter a person?

20. What name do the people of Oxford give to the agents of the General Oblation Board?

Jordan College

Test your knowledge of Lyra's adventures at home in Jordan College.

1. Which room does Lyra sneak into?

2. Who fills the last place at the dining table with Lyra and the Master?

3. What race of intelligent animals does Lyra say she'd like to meet if she went North?

4. Where does Lord Asriel take Lyra when his presentation is over?

5. Who is Lyra up on the College roof with?

6. Who are the Master and Fra Pavel talking about in the Retiring Room?

7. Where does Roger think the Gobblers take you?

8. How does Pan get into the garden with Lyra?

9. Which children are most likely to be taken by the Gobblers?

10. What kind of city is visible in the photogram shown by Lord Asriel?

11. What does Lyra do with her plum stones?

12. What does Lyra knock from Lord Asriel's hand?

13. What is the Master holding in his hand when he speaks to Lyra in her room?

14. Who is under the Jordan College dining table with Pantalaimon?

15. What does the Golden Monkey do to Pantalaimon: does he stroke his fur, hold his hand, or pull his tail?

16. Who does Mrs. Coulter tell Lyra is the only one that really, truly understood her as a child?

17. Why isn't Lyra ready to leave when Mrs. Coulter wants to take her?

18. Who tells Lyra off about the messy state of her knees and her hair?

19. What time of day is it when Lyra leaves Oxford with Mrs. Coulter: morning or evening?

20. Who wants to silence Lord Asriel?

Lyra's Friends

Test your knowledge of the amazing people and creatures that Lyra calls her friends.

1. Which Ice Bear was exiled from Svalbard?

2. What is Roger's surname?

3. Who is King of the Gyptians?

4. How does Roger describe the difference between himself and Lyra?

KING OF THE GYPTIANS

5. Who does Lyra say told her about the Gobblers taking the Gyptian children?

6. Where does Roger work?

7. Which man does Lyra meet for the first time in Trollesund?

8. How many balloons does Lee Scoresby's airship have?

9. Who meets Lyra when she is on the deck of the Gyptian ship?

10. Which of Ma Costa's sons has been taken by the Gobblers?

11. What does Farder Coram usually carry with him?

12. Who tells Lyra what has happened to Roger?

13. What is Lee Scoresby's main weapon – a sword, a gun or a crossbow?

14. Who is with Iorek when he arrives in Svalbard?

15. Who has a dæmon called Hester?

16. What job does Lee Scoresby do?

17. Who says "I have a contract with the child"?

18. What are Lyra and one of her friends doing on the roof of Jordan College?

19. What kind of dæmon does Ma Costa have?

20. What nickname does Iorek give to Lyra?

Lord Asriel and Mrs. Coulter

They're key characters, but how much do you know about them and what they're up to?

1. What part of the world did Lord Asriel travel to twelve months ago?

2. Why could Lyra go north with Mrs. Coulter: to be her assistant, to learn new languages, or to buy her new clothes?

3. What is in the tin that Lyra gives to Mrs. Coulter in Bolvangar?

4. What does Lord Asriel ask for from the Jordan College council?

5. What color is the dress Mrs. Coulter is wearing when she arrives at Jordan College?

6. Who, according to Lord Asriel, is "impossible to educate, a miscreant, and a liar"?

7. What is the name of Lord Asriel's dæmon?

8. Who does Lyra tell Roger she is spying on for her Uncle Asriel?

9. What story does Lyra tell about her Uncle and the guest from the Magisterium?

10. What word describes the color of the fur of Mrs. Coulter's dæmon?

11. What happens when Mrs. Coulter opens the tin that Lyra gives her at Bolvangar?

12. What connection does Lyra make between Mrs. Coulter and the Gobblers?

13. Whose permission does Lyra need to go with Mrs. Coulter?

14. When Pan finds Mrs. Coulter's list in her London home, what does Lyra think it is: a guest list, a shopping list, or a waiting list?

15. On Lyra's last day at Jordan College, why does Mrs. Coulter say they have to leave immediately?

16. How does Mrs. Coulter say that Lyra can contact Roger?

17. Why does Lyra say she needs to find Lord Asriel: to release him from his prison, to help with his experiments, or to give him the alethiometer?

18. Who tells Lyra that Dust is "none of your business"?

19. What can be seen in Asriel's photogram image?

20. What does the Master say he is concerned about with regard to Lyra going to London with Mrs. Coulter?

Movie Magic

How much do you know about the actors, characters, and creatures in this amazing movie?

1. Who plays Mrs. Coulter?

2. Which character is played by Sam Elliot?

3. Who is the voice for Pantalaimon?

4. Which character is played by Daniel Craig?

5. What is this Ice Bear's name (below)?

6. Who is Lyra talking to (above)?

7. What is the name of the actor who plays
   Fra Pavel: Simon McBurney or Jim Carter?

8. At the end of the film, who arrives just after Roger
   has disappeared?

9. Which part does Eva Green play in the movie:
   Ma Costa, Lyra, or Serafina Pekkala?

10. Where are Lyra and Roger when they're sitting
    on a roof eating plums?

11. What is the first name of the actress who plays Lyra: Dakota, Indiana, or Virginia?

12. Who is this character and what is his dæmon called (below)?

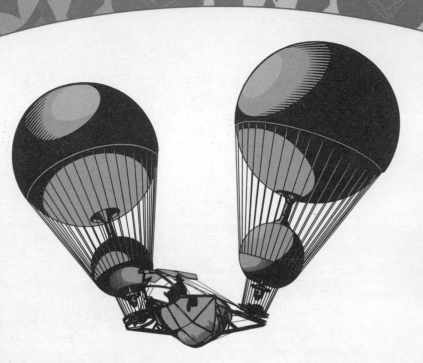

13. What is this (above)?

14. What nationality is Dakota Blue Richards?

15. What does Lord Asriel lose partway through the film: his hat, his beard, or his watch?

16. Which actor has said about the film, "Essentially it's a film about growing up, and how difficult that can be"?

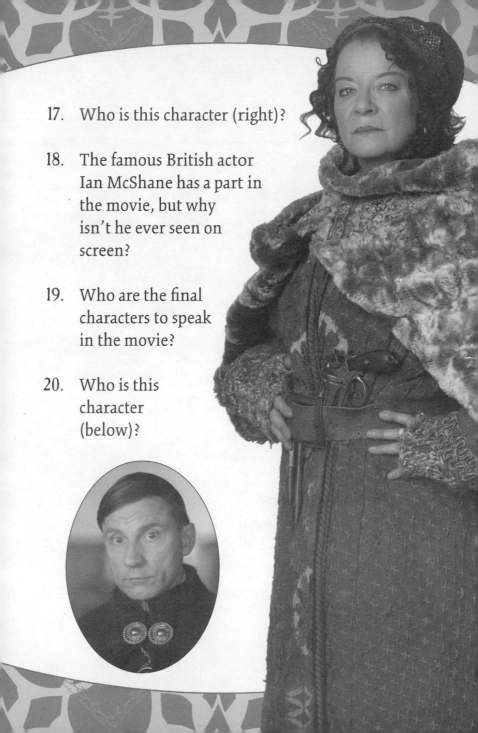

17. Who is this character (right)?

18. The famous British actor Ian McShane has a part in the movie, but why isn't he ever seen on screen?

19. Who are the final characters to speak in the movie?

20. Who is this character (below)?

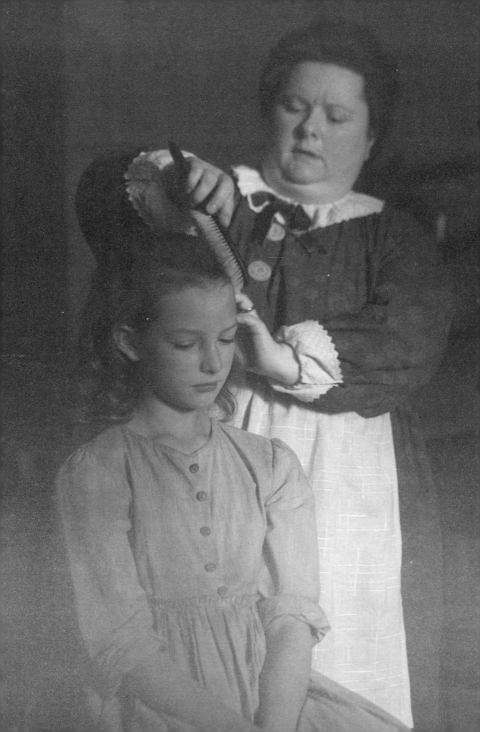

Short Cuts

These movie moments are over in a flash, but did they make a mark on your memory?

1. Who shoots at the Tartars from an airship?

2. Why does the Jordan scholar drop his books?

3. Who buys Lyra new clothes in London?

4. What is the name of the servant at Jordan College who looks after Lyra?

5. Are the Tartar soldiers bearded or clean-shaven?

6. At what time of day does Iorek Byrnison finish work in the sledge depot in Trollesund?

7. Why does Mrs. Lonsdale tell Lyra to come inside?

8. What dæmons do the Tartar guards have?

9. Who is the little boy Lyra and Pan find inside the Samoyed hut by the lake?

10. What dæmon does the Bolvangar official who greets Lyra have: a cheetah, an owl, or a praying mantis?

BOLVANGAR

11. How does Mrs. Lonsdale hurt Lyra?

12. Who does Mrs. Coulter hit in the face aboard the sky ferry on the way to Bolvangar?

13. Who shouts to Lyra to get off the roof?

14. What does the Bolvangar official give to the man who delivers Lyra to the Experimental Station?

15. What kind of dæmon belongs to the man who is killed after Lyra's capture in London?

16. What is Billy Costa's dæmon called?

17. What flies over Lyra and Iorek as they journey to the hut by the lake?

18. What dæmon does the Head Nurse at Bolvangar have?

19. What kind of dæmon does Lord Asriel's servant Thorold have?

20. Who is the man pictured with Roger (left)?

Dæmons

Humans and their dæmons are inextricably linked. How much do you know about these shape-changing creatures?

1. What form does Pantalaimon *not* take in the film: a cat, an ermine, or a wolf?

2. Who has a snow leopard as his dæmon?

3. What color is Pantalaimon when he takes the form of an ermine?

4. How do Pan and Salcilia greet each other when reunited in the Bolvangar canteen?

5. What does Asriel point out about Lyra's dæmon?

6. Who does Lyra ask whether it is "hard not having a dæmon?"

7. What flying creature does Pantalaimon take the form of when he spies for Lyra?

8. Who tries to stop Lyra entering the trapper's hut in the frozen North?

9. What kind of dæmon confronts Billy and Roger in Oxford?

10. Why are Lyra and Pan suspicious of the Golden Monkey in her London room?

11. What does Lyra throw at the Golden Monkey outside her bedroom door at Mrs. Coulter's home in London?

12. When one of the men pursuing Lyra in London is killed by a well-aimed arrow, what happens to his dæmon?

13. Who has a hawk as her dæmon?

14. What happens when the Golden Monkey's paw is trapped in a window?

15. Where is Pan when Lyra awakes after the intercision ordeal?

16. What does the Golden Monkey find in Lyra's room in London?

17. Who thinks Lyra is Iorek Byrnison's dæmon?

18. What happens to Billy Costa's dæmon at the beginning of the movie?

19. Which Ice Bear would like to have his own dæmon?

20. What is the first question Lyra is asked when she is taken to Bolvangar?

Eagle Eyes

Here's a real test – were you paying close enough attention to the movie's tiny details?

1. What color is Lee Scoresby's hair?

2. What does Fra Pavel tip into the decanter of wine?

3. What does Lyra destroy at Bolvangar?

4. What is inside the wooden box brought to Mrs. Coulter?

5. Who does Lyra shake hands with when they first meet on the Gyptian ship?

6. Whose portrait hangs on Mrs. Coulter's wall?

7. What does the scholar at Jordan College drop?

8. What does the Master of Jordan take out of the wardrobe in the Retiring Room?

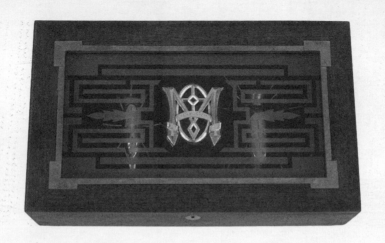

9. What hits the Jordan scholar on the head?

10. What is intercision?

11. What is there a picture of on the wall of the Bolvangar canteen?

12. What color is the woolen coat that Lyra is given by Ma Costa?

13. What kind of weapon is used by a Gyptian fighter to save Lyra from the Gobblers in London?

14. How does Lyra hurt the Golden Monkey when she escapes from Mrs. Coulter in London?

15. What happens when Iorek Byrnison attacks a Tartar soldier's wolf-dæmon?

16. What is King Ragnar wearing when Lyra first meets him?

17. Who else is in the ship's cabin when Lyra is introduced to John Faa?

18. What is Lyra doing when she meets Lee Scoresby?

19. What color is Serafina Pekkala's hair: dark, blonde, or red?

20. What is the name of the large, ocean-going Gyptian ship?

THE
Alethiometer

How much do you know about Lyra's amazing truth-telling device?

1. Where does the alethiometer get its name from?

2. How many needles and hands are on the alethiometer's dial?

3. What does Lyra carry the alethiometer in: her pocket, a leather satchel, or a backpack?

4. Who entrusted the Master of Jordan College with the safe-keeping of the alethiometer?

5. Who searches Lyra's room in London to find the alethiometer?

6. What does the alethiometer tell Lyra when she consults it at Bolvangar?

7. Why can't Farder Coram teach Lyra to read the alethiometer: because she has to learn for herself, because it will only share its secrets with one person, or because the art of reading it was jealously guarded?

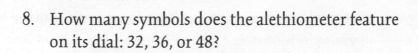

8. How many symbols does the alethiometer feature on its dial: 32, 36, or 48?

9. What symbol is combined with the hourglass symbol on the alethiometer: lightning, a skull or a candle?

10. What does Lyra give to Mrs. Coulter instead of the alethiometer?

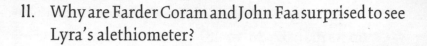

11. Why are Farder Coram and John Faa surprised to see Lyra's alethiometer?

12. Where does Lyra hide the alethiometer in Mrs. Coulter's London home?

13. Who is Lyra particularly keen to keep the alethiometer away from?

14. What does Lyra tell King Ragnar that dæmons use the alethiometer for: to keep watch over their human, to see into other worlds, or to see the truth in their own eyes?

15. How does Lyra use the alethiometer to help Iorek Byrnison in Trollesund?

16. What shocking news does the alethiometer give Lyra about Roger?

17. What is the alethiometer also known as?

18. How does Lyra move the alethiometer's hands?

19. What does Lyra say the alethiometer is when Ragnar first sees it?

20. What does Pan turn into to allow him to get a closer first look at the alethiometer in London?

Gyptians and Witches

See how much you know about these courageous characters.

1. Who rescues Lyra from the Gobblers' net after she's caught in London?

2. Does Serafina become Lyra's friend or enemy?

3. What weapon does Serafina carry?

4. Who is Ma Costa's youngest son?

5. Which two Gyptian elders is Lyra introduced to on the ship?

6. What does Lyra first do when she meets John Faa?

7. Whose barge does Lyra travel on after she is rescued in London?

8. What are the Gyptians looking at when Lyra arrives on the *Noorderlicht*?

9. What does Lyra show to Farder Coram and John Faa on the Gyptian ship?

10. Who tells Lyra to "hold the question in your mind, but lightly, like it was something alive" when using the alethiometer?

11. How do Gyptians usually travel: by sky ferry, boat, sledge, or carriage?

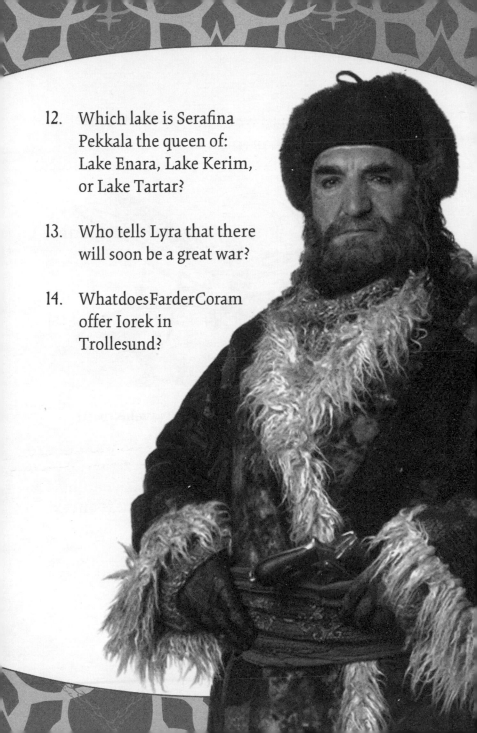

12. Which lake is Serafina Pekkala the queen of: Lake Enara, Lake Kerim, or Lake Tartar?

13. Who tells Lyra that there will soon be a great war?

14. WhatdoesFarderCoram offer Iorek in Trollesund?

15. What gets dropped when the spy-flies attack Lyra on the Gyptian ship?

16. Who leads the Gyptians as they travel North?

17. Who traps a spy-fly under a glass?

18. Who does Lyra cry to for help when she is carried off from the Gyptian camp?

19. How do the Gyptians travel from London?

20. Who does John Faa say has been "a friend of the Gyptians for many a year"?

Super Science

See how you measure up in the perplexing world of particle metaphysics, photograms, and parallel universes.

1. What is the name of the particles that stream down from the sky in Lord Asriel's photogram?

2. What is the name for the strange, mystical lights in the sky?

3. Who tells Lyra that the missing children are being taken to Bolvangar?

4. What is a dæmon mirror?

5. How does Dust get into humans?

6. What are contained on the glass spheres (right) that Asriel places in his projector?

7. What does one of the spy-flies use to attack Lyra?

8. Where is the gateway to the city in another world?

9. What holds Lee Scoresby's airship aloft?

10. Who does Lyra get into trouble with when she mentions "particles from space"?

11. What is Lord Asriel hoping to find out about in his travels around parallel universes?

12. What are spy-flies used for?

13. What can be seen outside the windows of Asriel's prison quarters in Svalbard?

14. Who does this character (below) work for?

15. Mrs. Coulter tells Lyra that she has met Lord Asriel at which scientific location?

16. What do the initials G.O.B. stand for?

17. What does Ragnar use to sharpen his claws?

18. What are the main weapons used by the witches?

19. What does Asriel describe as "bigger and stronger than anything they could imagine"?

20. What is released during intercision?

Here and There

**Are you any good at geography?
Don't forget, this is Lyra's world, not yours!**

1. Where did Iorek Byrnison live before he was exiled?

2. In which city does Lyra live when we first meet her?

3. In what country is the port of Trollesund?

4. Where do the Gobblers take the missing children: to the North, to the South, or to another world?

5. Where does Iorek live when Lyra first meets him?

6. What does Bolvangar mean: the Place of Death, the Place of Children, or the Place of Fear?

7. Where is the Kingdom of the Ice Bears?

8. On what transport is Lyra taken to Bolvangar?

9. What did Mrs. Coulter and Lord Asriel discuss on their supposed first meeting?

10. Where is Lyra going when she first travels in Lee Scoresby's airship?

11. How is Bolvangar guarded?

12. What town is Lyra in when she meets Lee Scoresby?

13. How do Lyra and Mrs. Coulter travel to London?

14. In which city is Jordan College?

15. Is Svalbard near the North Pole or the South Pole?

16. Where is this (below)?

17. Which country does the Gyptian ship sail to?

18. How do Lyra and Roger set off to find Lord Asriel in Svalbard?

19. What geographical feature prevents Iorek from catching up with Asriel?

20. Where is this battle taking place (below)?

In the North

Test your wits with these questions about Lyra's adventures in the frozen North.

1. What is Iorek Byrnison doing when Lyra first sees him: working, drinking, or eating?

2. Where do the children get taken when they reach the North?

3. What building does Lyra see as she is marched away by the bear soldiers at Svalbard?

4. What do Lyra and Pan find inside the Samoyed trapper's hut by the lake?

5. What does Lee Scoresby tell Lyra she should hire for her expedition with the Gyptians?

6. What name does Lyra give when she realizes the Bolvangar official doesn't know her?

7. What special skill helps Iorek Byrnison to earn a living in Trollesund?

8. What does King Ragnar really want?

9. What drink does Iorek Byrnison receive as payment for his work in Trollesund?

10. What do the children at Bolvangar do when they hear the fire alarm?

11. Who defends the children from the Tartars?

12. What does Lee Scoresby predict will be seen as an act of war in Svalbard?

13. What does Lyra pretend to be when she first meets King Ragnar?

14. What does Lyra use to answer King Ragnar's question about how he became king?

15. Who is King Ragnar's arch-enemy?

16. How did Ragnar become king?

17. Who does Lyra recognize among the children in the canteen at Bolvangar?

18. What does Lyra do as soon as she escapes from Mrs. Coulter in Bolvangar?

19. Why does Lyra need a quiet room, away from the children in the Bolvangar canteen?

20. Where does Iorek Byrnison work?

Lyra in London

**Can you remember what happened
to Lyra during her time in London?**

1. What is the main building that catches Lyra's
    eye as they fly into London?

2. Why is Lyra in London with Mrs. Coulter?

3. Where does Mrs. Coulter
    say that she and Lyra will
    be traveling to from
    London?

4. Who tells Lyra to take
    off her shoulder bag?

5. How do Lyra and
    Mrs. Coulter travel
    around in London?

6. Who is the lady who looks after Lyra when she is released from the Gobblers' net?

7. Who overpowers Pan in Mrs. Coulter's house?

8. Who tells Lyra that she must learn to control her dæmon?

9. Who travels in this vehicle (above)?

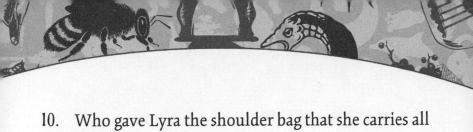

10. Who gave Lyra the shoulder bag that she carries all the time in London?

11. Whose shadow can Lyra and Pan see under her bedroom door?

12. How is Lyra captured after her escape from Mrs. Coulter's?

13. Who tries to stop Lyra and Pan escaping from Mrs. Coulter's apartment?

14. Where is Lyra when she is chased and caught?

15. Who do Lyra's captors work for?

16. What does Lyra hide under her pillow?

17. Where in Mrs. Coulter's home does Pan discover her special list of names?

18. Which dæmon tries to steal the alethiometer?

19. How do Pan and Lyra make their escape from Mrs. Coulter's apartment?

20. Who are the people who capture Lyra in the net?

Quote, Unquote

Were you listening carefully?
See if you can answer these tricky questions.

1. What does the Master say the alethiometer does?

2. What kind of kids, according to Roger, are taken by the Gobblers?

3. Who says to Lyra that "we help children grow up"?

4. Who told the Master that there are prophecies about Lyra?

5. What instructions does Asriel give to his his butler Thorold when Lyra and Roger arrive at his Svalbard prison?

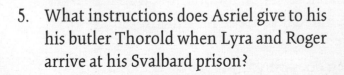

6. At Bolvangar, what does Lyra overhear has happened to Lord Asriel?

7. What does Lyra say the Gobblers do to you?

8. What kind of people, according to Lyra, are the Gobblers?

9. What does Serafina say is at stake in the coming war?

10. Who says Mrs. Coulter is "ghoulish"?

11. Does Mrs. Coulter say that Dust is good or bad?

12. Why does Lee Scoresby tell the Gyptians to be careful with his airship on the journey North?

13. What does Pantalaimon think is in the large, decorated box in the Retiring Room?

14. Who does Billy Costa say he is looking for in the trapper's hut in the frozen North?

15. What favor does the Master ask of Lyra?

16. What does the Master say to the Librarian about Lyra and a "betrayal"?

17. What does Pan say about their planned trip to the North with Mrs. Coulter?

18. What does Asriel mean when he says he will "break the unbreakable"?

19. What does Ragnar ask Lyra in order to prove that she is truly Iorek's dæmon?

20. Who says he will master his fear when he becomes afraid?

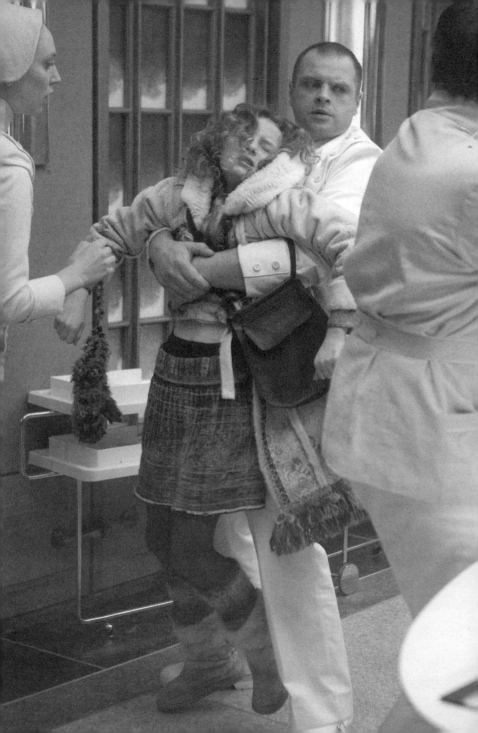

Super Test

Think you can answer some pretty tricky questions? See how many of these you get correct.

1. In Bolvangar, how does the doctor stop Lyra from fighting against her captors?

2. What is the Magisterium?

3. What did Lord Asriel investigate in the Arctic?

4. Why was Iorek Byrnison sent away from Svalbard?

5. Which Gyptian elder has white hair and a beard and sometimes wears a hat?

6. What color is Lee Scoresby's airship: blue, red, or silvery-gray?

7. What color is Pan when he appears at the table with Mrs. Coulter?

8. How do the Gyptians transport Lee Scoresby's airship on the way to the North?

9. Who wears a hooded leather jacket and goggles at the North Pole?

10. What subjects will Lyra have to learn to be Mrs. Coulter's assistant?

11. What is the Magisterial Seat in London?

12. Where is Iorek Byrnison's armor being kept?

13. Where does Lyra go to consult the alethiometer in Bolvangar?

14. What is a Panserbjørne's armor made from?

15. What is the name of Lord Asriel's servant?

16. Who does Lyra says is "rough and noble" like her Uncle Asriel?

17. Who is asleep in the belowdecks area of Lee Scoresby's airship when they travel to Svalbard?

18. What form does Pan take when he is lost with Lyra in the snow of Svalbard?

19. For what is the Master of Jordan College arrested by the Magisterial Police?

20. What kind of wine does Hunt serve to Lord Asriel?

What's in a Name?

There are all sorts of different character and place names in the movie. Can you remember them all?

1. What is Lyra's surname?

2. What do the Gyptians call non-Gyptians: land-lovers, land-lubbers, or land-lopers?

3. What is the name of the King of the Ice Bears?

4. How does Serafina introduce herself to Lyra?

5. Who is given the nickname Silvertongue?

6. What does Lord Asriel describe Lyra as: a spoilt brat, a dirty rat, or an alley cat?

7. What does Serafina call the Gobblers?

8. What do the witches of the North call the Experimental Station?

9. What are evil devices that the Magisterium sends after Lyra called?

10. How is Mrs. Coulter introduced to Lyra: as a friend of the College, as a sponsor, or as a friend of Lord Asriel?

11. Who taunts Iorek with the names "broken-hand, whimpering cub, and Soon-to-Die"?

12. What is the name of the man-servant who serves wine to Lord Asriel: Gerard, Hunt, or Parslow?

13. Who is John Faa's closest adviser?

14. What is Lee Scoresby's dæmon called?

15. What does the disapproving Pan describe Lyra as after their initial few days with Mrs. Coulter?

16. According to John Faa, who has been "hurt worse than most by the Gobblers"?

17. What is Roger's dæmon called?

18. Which Gyptian leader has a long, black beard?

19. What is the name of the College where Lyra lives in Oxford?

20. What is John Faa's title?

Plot Puzzlers

A mixed bag of questions about characters and events in the world of *The Golden Compass*.

1. What is a dæmon?

2. Whose appearance saves Lyra and Pan from the intercision process?

3. Why is a Panserbjørne's armor so precious to them?

4. Who saves the children at Bolvangar when they are surrounded by Tartar guards?

5. Who arrives at Bolvangar to help the witches defend the escaping children?

6. Who stops Iorek from getting shot by the police?

7. Why does King Ragnar want his own dæmon?

8. What is cut away during intercision?

9. How does Lyra stop Lord Asriel from drinking the poisoned wine?

10. Which individuals are able to travel a great distance away from their dæmons?

11. Who is endebted to Lyra?

12. Who wasn't allowed to see her own daughter for many years?

13. How does Lyra escape from Mrs. Coulter at Bolvangar?

14. What is released when a dæmon is cut from a person?

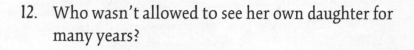

15. What does Lyra promise if Roger gets taken by the Gobblers?

16. Who says "a bear's armor is his soul"?

17. What is Billy Costa looking for when he is found inside the hut?

18. What does Lyra say she feels towards the Golden Monkey?

19. Who flies his own personal airship?

20. Who left Lyra in the care of Jordan College?

Quickfire Round

Answer these questions as fast as you can – some are truly easy, some are a little more tricky...

1. What does Lyra do to the Tartar guards as a sign of defiance?

2. What gets its name from the Greek word "alethia," meaning truth?

3. Who is Fra Pavel is trying to poison?

4. Who gets hit by Lyra and Roger's plum stones?

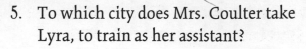

5. To which city does Mrs. Coulter take Lyra, to train as her assistant?

6. Who was Iorek's father?

7. Which of the bears loses the chainmail from his stomach armor during their fight – Ragnar or Iorek?

8. What item does Mrs. Coulter want from Lyra?

9. Where does Lyra hide in the Retiring Room?

10. How many spy-flies are in Mrs. Coulter's box?

11. Where do Lyra and Pan hide when Mrs. Coulter enters the dining room at Bolvangar?

12. Who works at the sledge depot behind Einarsson's bar?

13. Who does Lyra want to rescue from the Gobblers?

14. What does Lyra usually wear on her feet at Jordan College: sneakers, leather boots, or shoes?

15. Where are Lyra and Pan put when they're taken to the operating room at Bolvangar?

16. Who gets thrown out of Lee Scoresby's airship in the snowstorm?

17. What is visible in the sky, through the Aurora, when Lyra tracks down Lord Asriel?

18. What form does Lord Asriel's dæmon take?

19. What is the symbol of the Magisterium?

20. What kind of dæmon does John Faa have?

Unleash Your Inner Dæmon

What kind of a person are you?
What forms would your very own dæmon take,
and what final form would it fix on?
Take this fun quiz to find out more about
your own inner dæmon...

1. Which of these describes you best?
   a) Quick-thinking, independent, and determined
   b) Home-loving, reliable, and easy-going
   c) Single-minded, intellectual, and a loner
   d) Free-spirited, quiet, and thoughtful

2. How would you describe your friendships?
   a) Fiercely loyal, friends for life
   b) Caring and loving, and lots of fun
   c) Superficial and ever-changing
   d) Always there for each other, no matter what

3. Where is your favorite place to be?
   a) Out and about, hanging out with my friends
   b) Tucked up indoors somewhere cozy
   c) Exploring somewhere unknown
   d) In the great outdoors, getting back to nature

4. What are you like at school?
   a) School's boring, I'd rather not be there
   b) School's fun, I enjoy seeing everyone
   c) School's okay, but I know as much as the teachers
   d) School's fine as long as I'm with my friends

5. What's your favorite kind of holiday?
   a) Skiing or doing water sports
   b) Lazing on a beach or by the pool
   c) Exploring a new city or visiting museums and ruins
   d) Anywhere with a kids' club to join

6. How many close friends do you have?
   a) Just a few, but we're really close
   b) I have lots of friends
   c) Maybe one best friend, but I'm not close to many people
   d) A wide circle of good, loyal friends

7. What do you do on weekends?
   a) Whatever I feel like doing at the time
   b) Watch TV, go to parties and play video games
   c) Make time for my hobbies
   d) Meet my friends and head into town

8. How do you feel when you walk into a party?
   a) Not bothered at all, parties are fun
   b) A bit nervous until I see someone I know
   c) I feel fine, as I know someone will come over to talk to me
   d) I don't really go to parties

9. What do you do if you know the answer in class?
   a) Wait to see if I get picked on for an answer
   b) Keep quiet in case I'm actually wrong
   c) Stick my hand up to give the answer
   d) Silently hope I don't get chosen to speak out loud

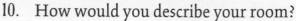

10. How would you describe your room?
    a) Minimalist – I don't have enough stuff to make a mess
    b) I've got loads of belongings, but I know where everything is
    c) There are things everywhere – tidying is a waste of precious time
    d) It's a great hidey-hole, no one is allowed in without my permission

11. Are you good at judging people's characters?
    a) No, my first impressions aren't always right
    b) No, I take everyone at face value
    c) Yes, I like to study other people and let them do the talking
    d) Yes, I've got an uncanny knack of getting it right the first time

12. Are you bossy?
    a) No, I let other people get on with it and do the same myself
    b) No, I'd rather have someone telling me what to do
    c) Yes, I'm always bossing people around
    d) I'm good at organizing but I'm not annoyingly bossy

13. How ambitious are you?
    a) Quite – once I'm on a mission I go for it
    b) Not at all – I just want an easy life
    c) Very – I want to be the best at what I do
    d) Not very – I'd rather be happy than successful, rich or powerful

14. Would you make a good teacher?
    a) I think so – I like helping other people
    b) No – I'm not clever enough really
    c) No – I'd lose my patience all the time
    d) Maybe – I'm patient and good with people

15. How lazy are you?
    a) Sometimes I can't be bothered to do things
    b) If I've got work to do, I'll do it
    c) I can't bear sitting around doing nothing
    d) I'm usually on the move doing something

16. How would you describe your personality?
    a) If I get sad I do something to take my mind off it
    b) I'm usually in a good mood
    c) I have major mood swings
    d) I'm never really happy or really sad

17. How would other people describe you?
    a) A bit wild but a really nice person
    b) Open and friendly
    c) People often think I'm rude or proud
    d) Shy and hard to get to know at first

18. Do you often tell lies?
    a) Yes, I just can't help it sometimes
    b) No, I get caught out when I try
    c) Only if it serves a purpose at the time
    d) No, honesty is something I really value

19. What would be your most embarrassing moment?

    a) It would take something really awful – I don't get embarrassed easily
    b) Being made to look stupid, like having a joke played on me
    c) Getting my facts wrong in front of other people
    d) Being scared in public – I like to put on a brave face

20. Would you spend your last $10 on cheering someone up?
    a) Yes, no problem – it would make me happy
    b) I'd rather spend my money on others anyway
    c) I doubt it – I don't know anyone I like that much
    d) There are only certain people I'd be prepared to do that for

21. Have you ever cheated in an exam?
    a) Yes – it just seemed easiest at the time
    b) No – I'm too scared of being found out
    c) I would if I needed to, but I've never actually needed to
    d) Not for myself, but I'd let others copy my work

22. Have you ever forgotten your best friend's birthday?
    a) No – I always remember
    b) No, I love buying presents for everyone!
    c) Yes – I've got more important things on my mind
    d) No, although I don't always buy conventional presents

23. Which of these is your favorite?
    a) Forests
    b) The countryside
    c) Mountains
    d) Oceans

24. Where do you get your spending money from?
    a) I'm always doing odd jobs to earn a bit of money
    b) I've got a Saturday job – it's actually good fun
    c) I work whenever and wherever I can to earn myself extra cash
    d) I get pocket money (with some extra from my grandparents if I'm lucky)

25. You've been invited to a party but your parents won't let you go. What do you do?
    a) Go into a massive sulk and plan how to sneak out
    b) Invite all your friends round to your house instead
    c) Pay no attention and go anyway, at the risk of being grounded
    d) Figure that they've got your best interests at heart and stay home

26. Someone pushes in front of you in a line. What do you do?
    a) Stand your ground and don't let them get away with it
    b) Scowl and moan but don't actually say anything directly
    c) Take no notice – it really doesn't matter to you
    d) Show them up in front of your friends

27. Do you struggle to make other people understand your ideas?
    a) Not really, I'm pretty clear when I'm explaining something
    b) No, I just find different ways of explaining them
    c) Yes – sometimes people just don't get it
    d) No, I'm good at working in a group

28. Where would you like to go on a date?
    a) Somewhere I've never been before
    b) A burger bar or pizza place
    c) An upmarket restaurant
    d) Somewhere romantic and quiet

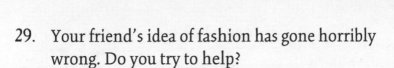

29. Your friend's idea of fashion has gone horribly wrong. Do you try to help?
    a) I'd hint at some new ideas but not make an issue of it
    b) I'd head straight to the shops and point out some better options
    c) I'd come straight out and say what was awful
    d) Fashion's not my thing, so who am I to judge?

30. Could you spend a day without your mobile phone?
    a) Yes, the peace would be welcome
    b) No – I'm always texting or talking
    c) Yes – unless I needed it for an emergency
    d) Easily – I'm usually with the people I want to talk to, anyway

So, what's your dæmon?
Turn the page to find out. . . .

Mostly A's

You've got a lot in common with Lyra, so it wouldn't be surprising for you to end up with a dæmon like Pan. Before it settles, your dæmon would switch rapidly, always reacting to the situation you're in. Whether it's a wildcat to scare your enemies, an eagle to soar to safety, or a polecat when you're on the defensive, your dæmon is ever-practical. It might not always be obedient to your thoughts and desires, though; as a nocturnal mammal, a hedgehog is a great form for your dæmon to take when it doesn't want you to sleep!

Although you have a wild side, your dæmon can show your softer side, too. Pan's favorite sleeping form is an ermine, and that would suit you perfectly – beautiful to look at, soft and cuddly, but with a free spirit that just can't be tamed.

Your dæmon, just like you, will be quick-thinking and imaginative. First, a mouse, to creep into small places or get up close to study details; next, a moth, a cunning disguise and a great way to conceal inner thoughts and feelings; change again, and it will be a lion, fiercely and undeniably protective and ready to fight. Once settled, your dæmon would most likely take the form of something sleek, swift, sharp-witted, and striking to look at. Take your pick – do you fancy a wildcat, a cheetah, or an ermine as your soul and life-companion?

Mostly B's

You're a home-loving person, and your dæmon will always reflect that. What isn't for certain is whether you're an independent sort, or happy to follow someone's lead. Your dæmon would most likely be a domesticated animal, like a cat, dog or even a rabbit. If you're meek and timid, expect it to settle as a rabbit; on the other hand, if you're self-contained and like the finer things in life, you'll no doubt end up with a cat by your side. Many people in this group are placid and reliable, and are suited to different kinds of dog-dæmon. Trot along with a terrier by your side, reflecting your simple but happy outlook on life, or become a servant with your own trusty serving dog as dæmon.

There are some in this group who are home-loving but not domesticated. If you like the outdoor life, but aren't too adventurous, you could end up with a dæmon that settles as a squirrel or a rat. These dæmons, like their humans, are industrious and swift, full of energy that is channelled into everyday tasks. Not for you the high-and-mighty life of an intellectual or an adventurer!

If thinking really isn't your strong point, then expect to have a homely bird as your dæmon. Sparrows are often found with humans who are friendly and inquisitive but not overly-intelligent, and a hen is a great dæmon for someone who is more interested in pecking at the minute details of everyday life than studying the grand questions of existence!

Mostly C's

Whatever form your dæmon takes, expect the unexpected! You're in line for a creature that is exotic or unusual. You stand out from a crowd and so will your dæmon. Not all exotic creatures are lovable, so don't be surprised if yours reflects your standoffish, even hostile, attitude to others. Maybe you're best suited to a snake or a lizard? Both of them have a bad reputation, but it's up to you whether you live up to that, or choose to focus on the more positive aspects of your character. You're almost certainly cool-headed, resilient, and brilliant when you're defending your own thoughts, ideas, or actions.

Some of the likely dæmons in this group are strikingly beautiful – but beware! That doesn't always suggest someone who is beautiful on the inside. Take, for example, Asriel's snow leopard and Mrs. Coulter's Golden Monkey. They are both fine creatures, but each has a wicked side. If you find yourself thinking sly thoughts, or sneaking around behind people's backs, you may well end up with a similar monkey-dæmon. Of course, a snow leopard is a rare and much-admired creature – but not renowned for being friendly or following another's lead. Does that sound like you?

Your dæmon form may be a surprise when it finally settles. Who would expect a pelican, a marmot, a macaw, or a chameleon? This kind of dæmon is usually associated with an independent thinker such as a scholar, or someone who is prepared to stand out in society.

Mostly D's

Many people in this group will have a bird as their dæmon – a sign of their free spirit and restless nature. Like the Gyptians, you're a wanderer and find it hard to settle. You may well end up with a striking bird-dæmon such as a hawk or a crow, showing strength of character and an admirable will to succeed.

For those of you who feel in harmony with nature and have a strong sense of belonging to a particular clan, it's also likely that your dæmon will reflect
these values. This kind of dæmon roams free, but is happy to be part of your chosen group or family.
The group spirit is very strong with you, but be careful to choose a group with the right sense of purpose. Like the Tartars, people with a wild or vicious side to their character could end up with a wolf-dæmon. If you're sure you're not wicked, but still feel the urge to stay on the fringe of society,
then a fox is a more likely dæmon for you.

Lee Scoresby also falls into this category, so
maybe you too could have a hare as your dæmon?

This is a sign of a person who lives life in the wild and follows their own path through life, but doesn't seek confrontation and is approachable and appealing with a softer side to their character. Choose your path in life carefully. . . .

The Final Test

Here's one last quiz – you should know all there is to know about Lyra's world by now!

1. When was the alethiometer given to Jordan College: last week, six months ago, or many years in the past?

2. Why have some Gyptians been arrested by the Magisterium?

3. What job does Iorek Byrnison do for the townspeople?

4. Why was Lyra taken away from her real parents?

5. Who is Ragnar Sturlusson?

6. When they first reach the North, why does Lyra want to ride on Iorek Byrnison's back?

7. Who carries Pan to the operating room at Bolvangar?

8. What gives Lyra and her friends a bumpy ride in the airship as they approach Svalbard?

9. Who was the true heir to the Svalbard throne?

10. Why does Iorek Byrnison stay in Trollesund instead of hunting and fighting?

11. Who keeps Lee Scoresby company alongside his airship on the approach to Svalbard?

12. Who watches over Lyra when she leaves Oxford?

13. What color are the spy-flies?

14. When did Lord Asriel first set off for the Arctic?

15. Why does Lyra arrange for Iorek and Ragnar to fight each other?

16. What does Lord Asriel's dæmon hold in her mouth as Asriel prepares his machine?

17. What does Asriel do to Roger's dæmon?

18. What does Mrs. Coulter suggest to Lyra when they meet over dinner at Jordan College?

19. What does Mrs. Coulter say the Ice Bears are called in the North?

20. How does Lyra find out where Iorek Byrnison's armor is?

Answers

Lyra's World

1. A dæmon
2. Uncle Asriel
3. Pantalaimon (or "Pan" for short)
4. She says that they died in an airship accident
5. She was just a baby
6. Ice Bears or Armored Bears
7. A Golden Monkey
8. The King of the Gyptians
9. Hunters and marauders in the North
10. At the age of puberty
11. An armored Ice Bear living in Trollesund
12. Sky-iron
13. Roger Parslow
14. Brytain
15. Hundreds of years
16. Lees Scoresby
17. In the North
18. It is Lyra, using a false name at Bolvangar
19. Through their dæmon
20. The Gobblers

Jordan College

1. The Retiring Room
2. Mrs. Coulter
3. The Ice Bears
4. Into the College garden
5. Her friend, Roger
6. Lord Asriel
7. Down to Hell
8. Lord Asriel's dæmon carries him in his mouth
9. Gyptians, poor children, orphans, servants, and market-workers
10. A city in another world
11. She spits them out off of the roof
12. A glass of poisoned wine
13. A little leather satchel
14. Mrs. Coulter's dæmon – the Golden Monkey
15. He strokes Pantalaimon's fur
16. Her dæmon
17. She hasn't said goodbye to Roger
18. Mrs. Lonsdale
19. Morning
20. Fra Pavel

Lyra's Friends

1. Iorek Byrnison
2. Parslow
3. John Faa
4. He says he's just a servant, but she's a lady
5. Billy Costa
6. In the kitchens at Jordan College
7. Lee Scoresby
8. Two
9. The witch, Serafina Pekkala
10. Billy
11. His walking stick
12. Ma Costa and John Faa
13. A gun
14. Roger
15. Lee Scoresby
16. He's an aeronaut
17. Iorek Byrnison
18. Eating plums and talking
19. A hawk
20. Lyra Silvertongue

Lord Asriel and Mrs. Coulter

1. The Arctic
2. To be her assistant
3. The captive spy-fly
4. Money (funding)
5. Gold
6. Lyra
7. Stelmaria
8. The Gobblers
9. She says her Uncle gave the man a hard look, and he fell dead on the spot
10. The fur is "Golden"
11. A spy-fly attacks Mrs. Coulter and the Golden Monkey, allowing Lyra and Pan to escape
12. Mrs. Coulter is running the Gobblers
13. The Master of Jordan College
14. "One of her stupid guest lists."
15. The Magisterial sky ferry is about to take off
16. She can write to him, and send him a photogram
17. To give him the alethiometer
18. Her Uncle Asriel
19. A man and his dog-dæmon, and particles in the air (Dust)
20. He is unsure it is what Lord Asriel would want for Lyra's education

Movie Magic

1. Nicole Kidman
2. Lee Scoresby
3. Freddie Highmore
4. Lord Asriel
5. Ragnar Sturlusson
6. Iorek Byrnison
7. Simon McBurney
8. Mrs. Coulter
9. Serafina Pekkala
10. Jordan College in Oxford
11. Dakota
12. Lee Scoresby, Hester
13. Lee Scoresby's airship
14. British
15. His beard
16. Daniel Craig
17. Ma Costa
18. He's the voice of King Ragnar Sturlusson
19. Lyra and Pantalaimon
20. Fra Pavel

Short Cuts

1. Lee Scoresby
2. He is hit on the head by Lyra's plum stone
3. Mrs. Coulter
4. Mrs. Lonsdale
5. They are bearded
6. Sunset
7. The Master has invited Lyra for dinner
8. Wolves
9. Billy Costa
10. A praying mantis
11. By brushing out the tangles in her hair
12. The Golden Monkey
13. Mrs. Lonsdale
14. Several heavy coins
15. A fox
16. Ratter
17. Witches
18. A dog (terrier)
19. A pinscher dog
20. Asriel's servant, Thorold

Dæmons

1. A wolf
2. Lord Asriel
3. White
4. They touch noses
5. He notes that it still changes shape, and hasn't settled yet
6. Iorek Byrnison
7. A bird
8. Pantalaimon
9. A Golden Monkey
10. He keeps looking towards her pillow beneath which the alethiometer is hidden
11. Her satchel
12. The dæmon disappears
13. Ma Costa
14. Mrs. Coulter cries out in pain
15. Snuggled up with her in the form of a cat
16. The alethiometer
17. Ragnar Sturlusson
18. She is captured by the Golden Monkey
19. King Ragnar Sturlusson
20. She is asked if her dæmon settled into one form yet

Eagle Eyes

1. He has long white hair
2. White powder (poison)
3. The intercision machine
4. Two spy-flies
5. John Faa
6. A portrait of Mrs. Coulter and the Golden Monkey
7. A pile of books
8. His academic robes
9. Lyra's plum stone
10. The process of cutting the human-dæmon bond
11. A tropical island
12. Purple
13. A bow and arrow
14. She closes the window on his paw
15. The dæmon disappears and the soldier dies
16. Jewels and golden claw decorations
17. Ma Costa, Farder Coram, and the chiefs of the Gyptian families
18. Reading the alethiometer
19. She has dark hair
20. The *Noorderlicht*

The Alethiometer

1. It's from "alethia," the Greek word for truth
2. One needle and three hands
3. A leather satchel
4. Lord Asriel
5. The Golden Monkey
6. It tells Lyra not to let Mrs. Coulter get hold of it (the alethiometer) or they'll die
7. He says the art of reading it was jealously guarded
8. 36 symbols
9. A skull
10. The captive spy-fly
11. They thought that all the alethiometers had been destroyed by the Magisterium
12. Under her pillow in her bedroom
13. Mrs. Coulter
14. To see the truth in their own eyes
15. The alethiometer reveals the location of Iorek's armor
16. That Lord Asriel is going to hurt him
17. The Golden Compass
18. By turning the three small knobs on the side of the device
19. A dæmon mirror
20. A mouse

Gyptians and Witches

1. Ma Costa and her sons
2. She becomes Lyra's friend
3. A cloud pine bow
4. Billy
5. John Faa and Farder Coram
6. She curtseys
7. The Costas' barge
8. They are looking at charts and maps
9. The alethiometer
10. Farder Coram
11. They usually travel by boat
12. Lake Enara
13. Serafina Pekkala
14. Employment
15. The alethiometer

16. John Faa
17. Farder Coram
18. Iorek Byrnison
19. By barge
20. Lord Asriel

Super Science

1. Dust
2. The Aurora (or the Northern Lights)
3. Serafina Pekkala
4. It's the name Lyra gives to the alethiometer when she tries to persuade Ragnar that she is Iorek's dæmon
5. Through their dæmon
6. Three-dimensional photogram images
7. A deadly spike mounted on its head
8. In the sky at the North Pole
9. Gas-filled balloons
10. Mrs. Coulter
11. He wants to find out more about Dust
12. They are used to retrieve objects and to track down the enemies of the Magisterium
13. The Aurora (the Northern Lights)
14. The Magisterium
15. The Royal Arctic Institute
16. General Oblation Board
17. Rock
18. Bows and arrows
19. Dust
20. Huge amounts of energy

Here and There

1. Svalbard
2. Oxford
3. Norroway
4. To the North
5. Trollesund
6. The Place of Fear
7. Svalbard
8. On a sledge
9. The political structure of the Ice Bears of Svalbard
10. To Svalbard
11. By a regiment of Tartars with wolf-dæmons
12. Trollesund
13. In a Magisterial sky ferry
14. Oxford
15. The North Pole
16. London
17. Norroway
18. In Lee Scoresby's airship
19. A thin ice bridge that won't hold his weight
20. The Gyptian camp in the North

In the North

1. He is eating a lump of meat
2. A place called the Experimental Station, or Bolvangar
3. The ice palace of King Ragnar
4. A boy whose dæmon has been cut away (Billy Costa)
5. An aeronaut and an Armored Bear
6. Lizzie Brooks
7. His metal-working abilities
8. A dæmon of his own
9. Whisky
10. Put on their warm clothes, ready to escape
11. Iorek, the witches, and the Gyptians
12. The return of Iorek Byrnison
13. Iorek's dæmon
14. The alethiometer
15. Iorek Byrnison
16. He poisoned the old king and then beat his heir, Iorek, in single combat
17. Roger Parslow
18. Lyra sets off the fire alarm
19. To consult the alethiometer
20. At the sledge depot behind Einarsson's bar, in Trollesund

Lyra in London

1. The Magisterial Seat
2. To train as her assistant
3. The North
4. Mrs. Coulter
5. By Magisterial carriage
6. Ma Costa
7. The Golden Monkey
8. Mrs. Coulter
9. Lyra and Mrs. Coulter
10. The Master of Jordan College
11. The Golden Monkey's shadow
12. She is caught under a net
13. The Golden Monkey
14. In a warehouse in the London Wharflands
15. The General Oblation Board
16. The alethiometer
17. In the wastepaper basket
18. The Golden Monkey
19. They leave via Lyra's bedroom window
20. Gobblers

Quote, Unquote

1. He says it tells the truth
2. Poor kids and ophings (orphans) and servant kids
3. The official that greets Lyra when she arrives at Bolvangar
4. The witches
5. To run a bath, prepare some food, and then let Roger go to bed
6. She hears that Asriel has been arrested and is being held in Svalbard under sentence of death
7. She says that they take children to a farm to fatten them up, ready to be eaten
8. Cannaboles (or cannibals)
9. She says that the Magisterium seeks to control "nothing less than free will."
10. A doctor at Bolvangar
11. Bad – she says it's evil
12. Damaging the "finicky" machinery could cause a fire
13. He bets it's "a box full of none-of-your-business"
14. Billy is looking for Ratter, his missing dæmon
15. The Master asks Lyra to keep the alethiometer to herself, especially keeping it from Mrs. Coulter
16. He says that Lyra will one day make a "great betrayal"
17. Pantalaimon says that they're never going to go
18. Asriel plans to break the bond between a person and their dæmon with his intercision machine, using the energy released to create a gateway to other worlds
19. He asks her to tell him how he became the Bear King
20. Iorek Byrnison

Super Test

1. He captures Pan and holds on to him
2. The organization that runs Lyra's world
3. A phenomenon that's registered on Jordan College's Dawkins Particle-Scope
4. He fought Ragnar in single combat and was defeated
5. Farder Coram
6. Silvery-gray
7. White
8. By sledge
9. Lord Asriel
10. Mathematics, navigation, and celestial geography
11. It is the headquarters of the Magisterium
12. In the district office of the Magisterium in Trollesund
13. The senior dining room
14. Sky-iron from the falling stars that land in Svalbard
15. Thorold
16. Iorek Byrnison
17. Lyra (and Pan), Roger and Iorek
18. He hides in the hood of Lyra's coat in the form of a mouse
19. Heresy
20. A '99 Tokay

What's in a Name?

1. Belacqua
2. Land-lopers
3. Ragnar Sturlusson
4. As clan-queen of the witches of Lake Enara
5. Lyra, by Iorek
6. An alley cat
7. The child-cutters
8. Bolvangar, the Place of Fear
9. Spy-flies
10. As a friend of the college
11. Ragnar, during their fight
12. Hunt
13. Farder Coram
14. Hester
15. Mrs. Coulter's new pet
16. The Gyptians
17. Salcilia
18. John Faa
19. Jordan College
20. King of the Gyptians

Plot Puzzlers

1. A person's soul that lives outside their body in animal form
2. Mrs. Coulter saves Lyra and Pan
3. They consider their armor to be their soul
4. Iorek Byrnison
5. The Gyptians
6. Lee Scoresby
7. Bears don't have dæmons, and he wants to be like a human
8. A person's dæmon
9. She knocks the glass out of his hand
10. Witches
11. Iorek, because Lyra helped him to retrieve his armor
12. Mrs. Coulter
13. She tricks her into unleashing the captured spy-fly, which attacks Mrs. Coulter
14. The energy associated with Dust
15. That she will rescue him
16. Iorek Byrnison
17. His dæmon, Ratter
18. She hates him
19. Lee Scoresby
20. Her uncle (Lord Asriel)

Quickfire Round

1. She spits at them
2. The alethiometer
3. Lord Asriel
4. One of the Jordan scholars
5. London
6. The former King of the Ice Bears
7. Ragnar
8. The alethiometer
9. In a wardrobe
10. Two
11. Under the table
12. Iorek Byrnison
13. Roger Parslow
14. Leather boots
15. They are put into cages
    in the intercision machine
16. Lyra and Pan
17. A city
18. A snow leopard
19. A crest in the shape of an "M"
20. A crow

The Final Test

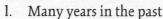

1. Many years in the past
2. For breaking into the office of records
3. He mends broken machinery and articles of iron, and lifts heavy objects
4. They weren't married when she was born
5. The King of the Ice Bears
6. To travel to the next valley to find the hut by the lake
7. The Head Nurse
8. A snow-squall
9. Iorek Byrnison
10. The local people took away Iorek's armor, so he cannot go to war
11. Serafina Pekkala
12. Ma Costa and the Gyptians
13. Metallic gold
14. Twelve months before his visit to Jordan College
15. To prevent Iorek being killed by Ragnar's sentries when he approaches the ice palace
16. Roger's dæmon, Salcilia
17. Asriel severs the dæmon from Roger using his intercision machine
18. She suggests that Lyra join her on a trip to the North
19. Panserbjørne
20. She uses the alethiometer